It's Time to Play!

Pre-Level 1

P1 PRE-LEVEL 1: ASPIRING READERS

- Short and simple texts with familiar themes and topics
- Concepts in text are reinforced by illustrations
- Simple sentence structure and repeated sentence patterns
- Easy vocabulary familiar to kindergarteners and first-graders

 LEVEL 1: EARLY READERS

 LEVEL 2: DEVELOPING READERS

 LEVEL 3: ENGAGED READERS

LEVEL 4: FLUENT READERS

studio fun
INTERNATIONAL

Studio Fun International
An imprint of Printers Row Publishing Group
A division of Readerlink Distribution Services, LLC
10350 Barnes Canyon Road, Suite 100, San Diego, CA 92121
www.studiofun.com

ISBN: 978-0-7944-4710-6
Manufactured, printed, and assembled in Shaoguan, China.
Second printing, November 2020. SL/11/20
24 23 22 21 20   2 3 4 5 6

It's time to play!

It's fun to play.

There are so many fun ways to play!

The swings are fun.

Swing in the air.

The sandbox is fun.
Dig in the dirt.

The slide is fun, too.
Climb up.

Slide down.

Jump rope is fun.
Jump!

Hopscotch is fun.
Hop!

Make-believe is fun, too.
ZOOM like an airplane!

GALLOP like a horse!

ROAR like a dinosaur!

BEEP like a truck!

Here's something else that's really fun!

Racing is fun.

Ready. Set. Go!

A jungle gym is fun, too.

Hide-and-seek is a fun game.

Simon Says is a fun
game, too.

Blowing bubbles is fun!

Popping bubbles
is a lot of fun.

POP!

Bouncing balls is a lot of fun, too.

BOUNCE!

The seesaw goes up
and down.

The horse goes back and forth.

The kite flies higher
and higher.

It's fun to ride a bicycle.

It's fun to draw, too.

It's fun to play!